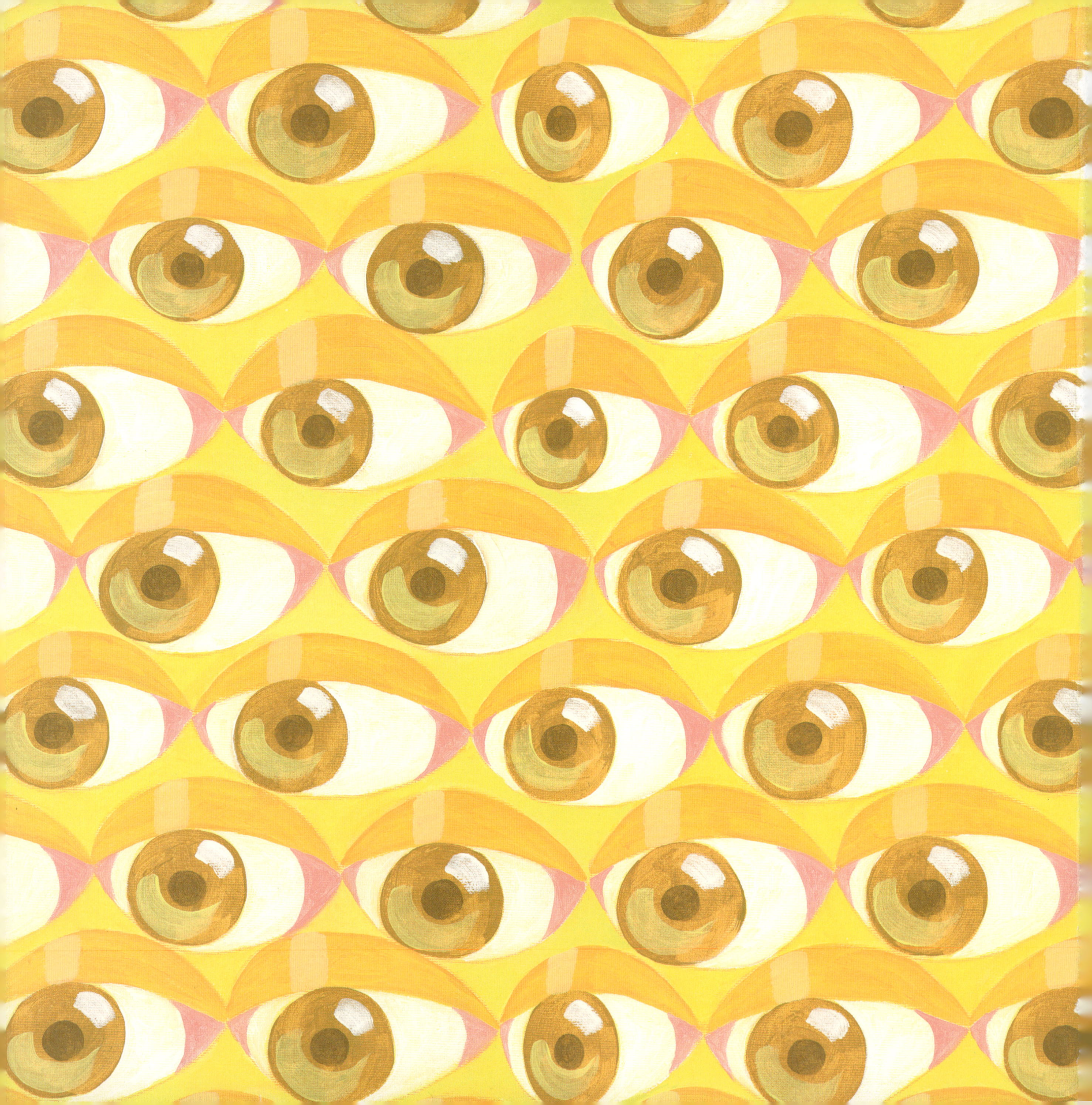

Special thanks to
Malka Carmi-Drori and Nadav Levi
for sharing their holiday memories

Reycraft Books
55 Fifth Avenue
New York, NY 10003

Reycraftbooks.com

Reycraft Books is a trade imprint and trademark of Newmark Learning, LLC.

Text © Reycraft Books

Illustrations and paintings © Eliahou Eric Bokobza

All rights reserved. No portion of this book may be reproduced, stored in a retrieval system, or transmitted in any form or by any means, electronic, mechanical, photocopying, recording, or otherwise, without written permission from the publisher. For information regarding permission, please contact info@reycraftbooks.com.

Educators and Librarians: Our books may be purchased in bulk for promotional, educational, or business use. Please contact sales@reycraftbooks.com.

This is a work of fiction. Names, characters, places, dialogue, and incidents described either are the product of the author's imagination or are used fictitiously. Any resemblance to actual persons, living or dead, is entirely coincidental.

Sale of this book without a front cover or jacket may be unauthorized. If this book is coverless, it may have been reported to the publisher as "unsold or destroyed" and may have deprived the author and publisher of payment.

Library of Congress Control Number: 2020925470

ISBN: 978-1-4788-7049-4

Printed in Dongguan, China. 8557/0221/17683

10 9 8 7 6 5 4 3 2 1

First Edition Hardcover published by Reycraft Books 2021

Reycraft Books and Newmark Learning, LLC support diversity and the First Amendment, and celebrate the right to read.

Photo Credits: Front Cover: Oscar Bjarnason/Getty Images; Page 4, 5: Kusska/Shutterstock; Page 6, 7: ziviani/Shutterstock; Page 8, 9: Westend61/Getty Images; Page 10, 11: SFIO CRACHO/Shutterstock; Page 12, 13, 30, 31: zhu difeng/Shutterstock; Page 20, 21: THINK A/Shutterstock; Page 32, 33: Seqoya/Shutterstock; Page 34, 35: FocusStocker/Shutterstock; Page 40: Provided by Wiley Blevins

Sunday with Savta

Eliahou Eric Bokobza | Wiley Blevins

Everyone gathered around to see her photo album.
And to hear her stories.

There were so many stories and so many people.
I couldn't get close.

"Don't worry, khamoodi," Savta said from across the room. "It's just the two of us on Sunday."

**Sunday with Savta.
What could be better?**

We started by hopping on the ferry to the Statue of Liberty. "Your Great Aunt Neshka came here years ago," said Savta. "But I wanted to go to Israel to live. That's where your mother was born. Come."

Savta pointed to a little museum near the river.

"I have a special gift for you."

We entered a long hallway.
"This way," Savta said. "Look!"

"What are these?" I asked.

"These are paintings of holidays.

Our holidays. Don't you know them?"
I shook my head.
"Oy," said Sayta. "I'm glad I'm here."

"This painting shows Pesach, or Passover.

That's when God freed the Israelites from slavery in Egypt long ago. When I was your age, my abba bought a carp to prepare gefilte fish for the holiday meal. But that year we didn't have a working refrigerator. So, you know what my dad did?"

"No," I whispered, leaning closer.

"He put the fish in the bathtub to keep fresh. No one could take a bath for three days. We smelled as bad as the fish that holiday!" Savta laughed so loud everyone stared.

"This is Sukkot," said Savta more softly. "I showed you the photo of the sukkah, or white tent, we built in my backyard this year, right?" I nodded.

"One year my brother, your Uncle Nadav, loved Sukkot so much he decided to surprise decorate the sukkah all by himself. This was something the whole family usually did. So, he climbed on a tall ladder. You can probably guess what happened next."

"He fell?" I asked.

"BOOM! Like a rock. He broke both his right leg and right arm. No yummy kreplach or kugel for him. He spent the entire holiday in the hospital."

Savta marched in place in front of the next painting. "What are you doing?" I asked, looking around.

"I can hear the music in my memory," she said.

"**Every Simchat Torah,** we would join in the parade marching through town. Someone would hold the Torah, our holy book, high in the air as we sang and danced. Kids and grown-ups. Boys and girls. All together. Now that's how you celebrate the most important book ever written."

With that, Savta and I marched into the next room.

There, we sat on a bench. Savta sighed. "Memories can tire you out."

"Look! It's Hanukah!" I said, pointing. "My favorite holiday."

"Mine, too," said Savta. "And not just for the eight days of presents and candle lighting. Each year I would watch my ima make the donuts. But, oh, how impatient I was to try the first one.

My mom never allowed anyone to eat them until she had squirted the jam inside and sprinkled powdered sugar on top. And she was right. They were perfect."

Savta grabbed my hand. "I wish I could have just one more."

"This looks like Halloween in New York," I said.

"Well, maybe," said Savta.

"We call it Purim. Kids love to dress up in costumes just like you do for Halloween."

"But it's not a holiday about ghosts and goblins, right?"

"Oh, no," said Savta. "It's about a queen named Esther. When I was a girl, I always knew my next year's costume."

"How?"

"My family didn't have a lot of money, so any Purim costume my big brother had I got the following year. I was the only girl cowboy and the only girl superhero and the only girl pirate.

But I'll never forget Purim when I was eight. I got a big box from my parents the day before. Inside was the perfect queen costume. Never worn. Just like I always wanted."

"He's planting a tree?" I asked as we stood in front of the next painting.

"**This is Tu Bishvat,** when we plant trees all over Israel. Once my parents took me to plant a baby tree in a Jerusalem forest. Next to my little tree, I put a sign so everyone would know this was my tree. I imagined years later how this baby tree would grow into a tall tree in a giant forest. I bet it's taller than both of us now!"

"Neither one of us is very tall," I reminded Savta.

"Oh, dear," said Savta. "Yom Kippur. The Day of Atonement."

I had no idea what atonement meant, but it didn't sound happy.

"This is the holiest day of the year for us Jews," said Savta. "It's when we ask for forgiveness. No one drives cars. There's no TV. Nothing. It's the quietest day of the year. Just wonderful."

"Then why do you look sad?" I asked, grabbing Savta's hand.

"On this day many years ago, I was looking out my window. Suddenly tanks and long lines of army cars raced by. We were being attacked on all sides. It was the start of what they now call the Yom Kippur War."

"What happened?" I asked.

"We won," Savta said. "Our little country won."

"And this painting?" I asked, hoping it would be a happier memory. "I see the flag of Israel on it."

"Yes. Blue and white.

This is Yom Ha-Atzmaut—the Israel Independence Day. Like your 4th of July. It's a day of great celebration and pride. Like all our holidays."

"In a little over a year when you're thirteen, you'll be celebrating your Bar Mitzvah," said Savta.

"In Israel."

"We can take a photo of just us two. For your photo album," I said. "You can put it next to **my bris photo**, when I was only eight days old. Like the boy in this painting."

Savta slowly nodded, then looked away.

It's been a year and a half since Savta's visit and we are finally in Israel. Mom. Dad. And me.

The Jerusalem heat slaps my face as we leave the taxi and walk up the hill. I think back to the day Savta and I went to the museum—the last time I saw her.

I remember Savta promised me a gift that day, but I never got one. "What did she want to give me?" I wonder. My mind floods with her stories. Smelly fish. Costumes. Yummy donuts. Trees and family.

Then I know.

Her stories.

I lean in and place a small stone on Savta's grave.

"I will tell your stories," I whisper.

"All of them. To everyone. Thank you, Savta."

"Now it's time to go see that tree of yours."

A Brief Look at Jewish Holidays and Important Celebrations

Rosh HaShanah (New Year)
Celebrates the first day on the Jewish calendar (usually in late September). Apples and honey are commonly eaten. A shofar, or ram's horn, is blown in the synagogue.

Yom Kippur (Day of Atonement)
This is a day of fasting (no eating) and prayer for forgiveness of all your sins during the year. Many people wear white on this day.

Sukkot
A harvest festival when families build and stay in a sukkah, or tent, outside.

Simchat Torah
Celebrates the Torah, or holy book for Jews. Families gather at the synagogue, roll up the Torah scrolls, and sing and dance.

Hanukah

This eight-day holiday celebrates the capture and dedication of the Jewish temple in Jerusalem. Potato pancakes, called latkes, and jelly donuts, called sufganiyot, are eaten. Each night a candle is lit on the special Hanukah menorah. Children play a game with a spinning top, called a dreidel.

Purim

Celebrates the Jews' escape from death thanks to the strength and intelligence of Queen Esther. Triangle-shaped pastries called hamantashen are eaten. People dress in costumes and twirl noisemakers.

Pesach (Passover)

Celebrates the Israelites' escape from slavery in Egypt as detailed in the book of Exodus. Jews eat no leavened bread, instead eating matzah—a flat unleavened bread. Families gather for a seder, a traditional meal with the reading of the biblical story.

Shabbat (Sabbath)

It's the holy day of rest observed each week. It begins around sundown on Friday and ends around sundown on Saturday. Traditionally, no work is done. The family gathers for a meal and special prayer. It's also when Jews go to their local synagogue.

Bar Mitzvah

This Jewish coming-of-age ritual for boys occurs on the boy's 13th birthday. For girls, the ritual is called Bat Mitzvah and occurs on the girl's 12th birthday.

Brit Milah (Bris)

This is the day a baby boy is circumcised by a rabbi, per Jewish tradition. It takes place on the 8th day of the boy's life.

Tu Bishvat (The New Year for Trees)

Traditionally on this day, the first fruits of the trees were given to the temple in Jerusalem. Now, it's a day to plant trees and think about the environment.

Lag B'Omer

This is a traditional day of mourning. People light bonfires, go on picnics or camping, and get their hair cut.

Shavuot

This harvest festival celebrates the giving of the Torah to Moses. The eating of dairy products is common. One popular traditional food is blintzes.

Yom Ha-Shoah (Holocaust Remembrance Day)

Honors Jewish resistance to the Nazi killing of Jews during World War II. In Israel an air raid siren blares for two minutes at 10:00 a.m. Everyone stops in place, gets out of their cars, and remembers those who died.

Yom Ha-Atzmaut (Israel Independence Day)

Celebrates the day the modern state of Israel was formed in 1948. Jews wave the Israeli flag, attend outdoor festivals and shows, and enjoy typical Israeli foods.

Eliahou Eric Bokobza

Eliahou Eric Bokobza was born in Paris, France, of Tunisian parents. When he was six his family immigrated to Israel, where he now lives. Trained as a pharmacist, he pursued his passion in art and is now one of the most recognized artists in Israel. His works are part of the permanent collection in the Knesset Parliament, the Israel Museum, and other museums worldwide.

Wiley Blevins

Wiley Blevins is a writer living in New York City. When he lived in Tel Aviv, Israel, he spent a lot of time in Bokobza's studio discussing his paintings. Wiley has collected several of Bokobza's works, including a painting that once hung in the Tel Aviv Museum of Art.